THE
KITCHEN KNIGHT

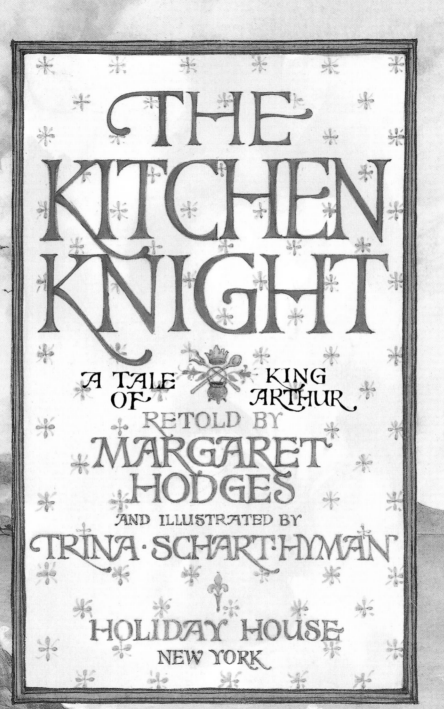

THE KITCHEN KNIGHT

A TALE OF KING ARTHUR

RETOLD BY

MARGARET HODGES

AND ILLUSTRATED BY

TRINA·SCHART·HYMAN

HOLIDAY HOUSE

NEW YORK

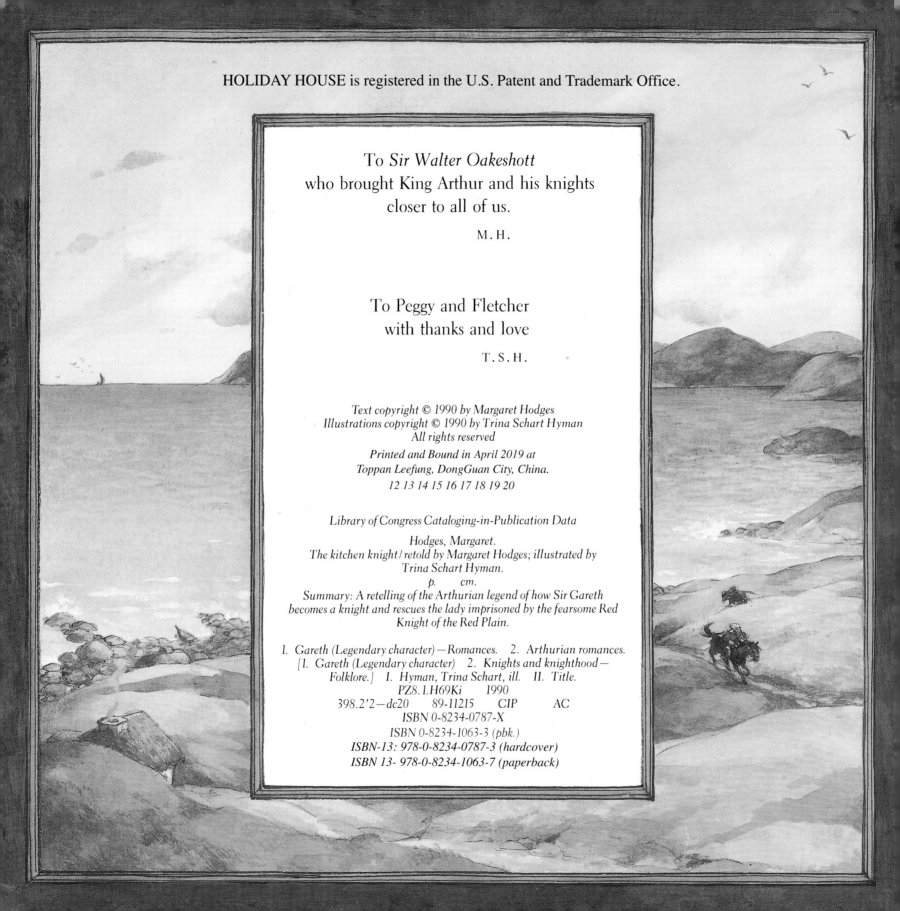

To *Sir Walter Oakeshott*
who brought King Arthur and his knights
closer to all of us.

M. H.

To Peggy and Fletcher
with thanks and love

T. S. H.

Text copyright © 1990 by Margaret Hodges
Illustrations copyright © 1990 by Trina Schart Hyman
All rights reserved
Printed and Bound in April 2019 at
Toppan Leefung, DongGuan City, China.
12 13 14 15 16 17 18 19 20

Library of Congress Cataloging-in-Publication Data

Hodges, Margaret.
The kitchen knight / retold by Margaret Hodges; illustrated by
Trina Schart Hyman.
p.   cm.
Summary: A retelling of the Arthurian legend of how Sir Gareth
becomes a knight and rescues the lady imprisoned by the fearsome Red
Knight of the Red Plain.

1. Gareth (Legendary character)—Romances.   2. Arthurian romances.
[1. Gareth (Legendary character)   2. Knights and knighthood—
Folklore.]   I. Hyman, Trina Schart, ill.   II. Title.
PZ8.1.H69Ki   1990
398.2'2—dc20   89-11215   CIP   AC
ISBN 0-8234-0787-X
ISBN 0-8234-1063-3 (pbk.)
ISBN-13: 978-0-8234-0787-3 (hardcover)
ISBN 13- 978-0-8234-1063-7 (paperback)

In the springtime, when the Round Table was in its glory, King Arthur always held a high feast. But before he sat down at the table, he liked to hear something new, or some adventure. Once, when he was waiting to keep the feast at a seaside castle, he looked from a window and saw in the courtyard a tall young man riding a poor horse and followed by a dwarf. The young man dismounted and the dwarf led the horse away.

Then the stranger came into the hall. He was a goodly young fellow. His manner was friendly, modest, and mild. He was big, broad in the shoulders, and handsome, the very sort to bring news of an adventure. So Arthur made him welcome to the feast and sat down at the table with all his knights around him.

"God bless you, King Arthur," said the young stranger, "and God bless the fellowship of the Table Round. I have come to ask you for three favors. Today I ask for the first. Give me meat and drink for one year. At the end of the year I will ask my other two favors."

"Granted," said Arthur, "for my heart tells me that you will prove to be a man of great worth. What is your name?"

"I cannot tell you," said the youth.

"A goodly young man like you does not know his own name?" said the king in jest. Then he told Sir Kay, his steward, to give the youth the best of meat and drink and all other things that a lord's son should have.

"There is no need for that expense," Kay said to himself. "A gentleman would have asked for a good horse and armor. This fellow is a peasant, as overgrown as a weed, and wanting nothing but meat and drink. He can work and eat in the kitchen. At the end of a year he will be fat as a hog."

Now Arthur's best knight, Sir Lancelot, was kind to the young man because of his own great gentleness and courtesy, while Sir Kay was always rude to the stranger. But the boy took his place in the kitchen and shared the work without complaint. When the kitchen lads competed in sports, the unknown youth was a winner. When the knights jousted, he was always watching.

So a year passed, and once again the king wished to hear of some adventure before he sat down at the springtime feast. Then there came a squire who said to the king, "Sir, you may sit down to eat, for here comes a lady with a strange adventure to tell."

At once, a proud lady came into the hall and said, "Sir, I have come to you because your knights are the noblest in the world. I ask one of them to help my sister, who is held prisoner in her castle."

"What is her name?" asked the king. "And where does she dwell?"

"I will not tell you," said the lady. "But the tyrant who holds her prisoner in her castle is Sir Ironside, the Red Knight of the Red Plain. He is evil, and as strong as seven men."

Then the tall kitchen boy stepped forward and knelt before the king. "Sir," he said, "I have been for twelve months in your kitchen and have had my meat and drink as you promised. Now I will ask my last favors. Let me have this adventure, and let Sir Lancelot ride after me. If I win my spurs, let him make me a knight."

The king was well pleased. "All this shall be done," he said.

But the lady cried, "For shame! Must I have a kitchen boy for my champion?" And she took her horse and rode off.

Then there came into the courtyard the same dwarf who had arrived with the stranger a year before. He was leading a fine horse which carried on its back a breastplate and sword. The kitchen boy took the sword and armor, and mounted the horse. Then he asked Sir Lancelot to follow, and without shield or lance rode after the lady. The dwarf rode behind.

Sir Kay rode after them and ordered them to stop, for he thought the kitchen boy unworthy to be the champion of so proud a lady. The boy rode on.

Sir Kay called angrily, "Fellow, do you not know my voice?"

The boy turned his horse and answered, "I know you for the most ill-mannered knight of King Arthur's court."

Kay put his spear in the saddle rest and rode straight upon him, and the kitchen boy came fast upon Kay with his sword in hand. He thrust Kay's spear aside and struck such a blow that Kay fell from his horse and lay stunned on the ground. Then the kitchen boy took Sir Kay's spear and shield. He put the dwarf on Kay's horse, mounted his own, and rode after the lady.

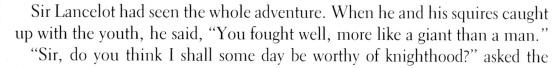

Sir Lancelot had seen the whole adventure. When he and his squires caught up with the youth, he said, "You fought well, more like a giant than a man."

"Sir, do you think I shall some day be worthy of knighthood?" asked the kitchen boy.

"You are worthy this day," said Lancelot. "I will knight you here and now. But first, tell me your name and family."

"I am Gareth of Orkney, from the islands far to the north, and I am nephew to the king," said the young man, "but the king must not know until I have truly won my spurs."

Then Lancelot dubbed Gareth a knight and returned to Arthur's court, while his squires had to carry Sir Kay on a shield.

Sir Gareth rode on and overtook the proud lady. "Is it you again?" she said. "You smell of the kitchen and your clothes are foul with kitchen grease under your armor. Do you think I like you better for wounding that knight? You did not fight fairly. Go away, you lubber, you turner of spits and washer of ladles."

"Madam," said Gareth, "say what you will, I shall fight against any knight who bars your way. I will follow this adventure to the end, or die in the attempt."

"You would not face the Red Knight of the Red Plain for all the soup in the kitchen," said she.

"I will try," he said.

At the day's end they came to a castle where a knight offered them good cheer and set a table for them. But the lady said, "This kitchen boy is more fit for pig-sticking than for sitting with a lady of high degree."

The knight of the castle was ashamed of her words. He took Gareth to another table and ate there with him, leaving the proud lady to sit by herself.

The next day Gareth rode on with her, and she never gave him a civil word. Then they came to a black field and saw a black hawthorn tree with a black banner and a black shield hanging on it. Beside the tree stood a great black horse covered with trappings of black silk. And on the horse sat a knight in black armor, barring the way.

"Lady," said he, "have you brought this knight to be your champion against me?"

"No," she said, "he is only a kitchen boy, and I would gladly be rid of him."

"Then I will take his horse and armor from him," said the knight in black armor. "It would be a shame to do more harm than that to a kitchen boy."

"I am about to cross your field," said Gareth. "Let us see if you can take my horse and armor." Then they rode against each other and came together with a sound like thunder. The knight in black armor smote Gareth with many strokes and hurt him full sore, but Gareth fought back and brought him to the ground. He won the black horse and the black armor, and rode after the lady.

"Away, kitchen boy," she said. "Out of the wind. The smell of your clothes offends me. Alas, that such a knave as you should fell so good a knight, and all by luck. But the Red Knight will kill you. Away, flee while you can."

"Lady," said Gareth, "you are not courteous to speak to me as you do. Always you say that I should be beaten by knights that we meet, but for all that, they lie in the dust."

Then they came to a meadow, new mown and full of blue pavilions. The lady said, "A noble knight comes in fair weather with five hundred knights to joust in this meadow. You had better flee before he sets upon you with all his knights."

"If he is noble, he will not set upon me with five hundred knights," said Gareth. "And if they come one at a time, I will face them as long as I live."

Then the lady was ashamed and said, "I pray you, save yourself while you can. You and your horse have fought hard and long, and you will have the hardest fight of all when we come to my sister's castle."

Gareth answered, "Be that as it may, I shall deal with this knight now, and we shall come to your sister's castle while it is still daylight."

"What manner of man are you!" said the lady. "Never did a woman treat a knight so shamefully as I have you, and you have always answered me courteously. Only a man of noble blood would do so."

He answered, "I am Gareth, the king's nephew. I ate my meat in his kitchen so that I might know who are my true friends, and I never minded your words, for the more you angered me, the better I fought."

"Alas," she said, "forgive me."

"With all my heart," said Gareth. "And now that we are friends, I think there is no knight living but I am strong enough to face him."

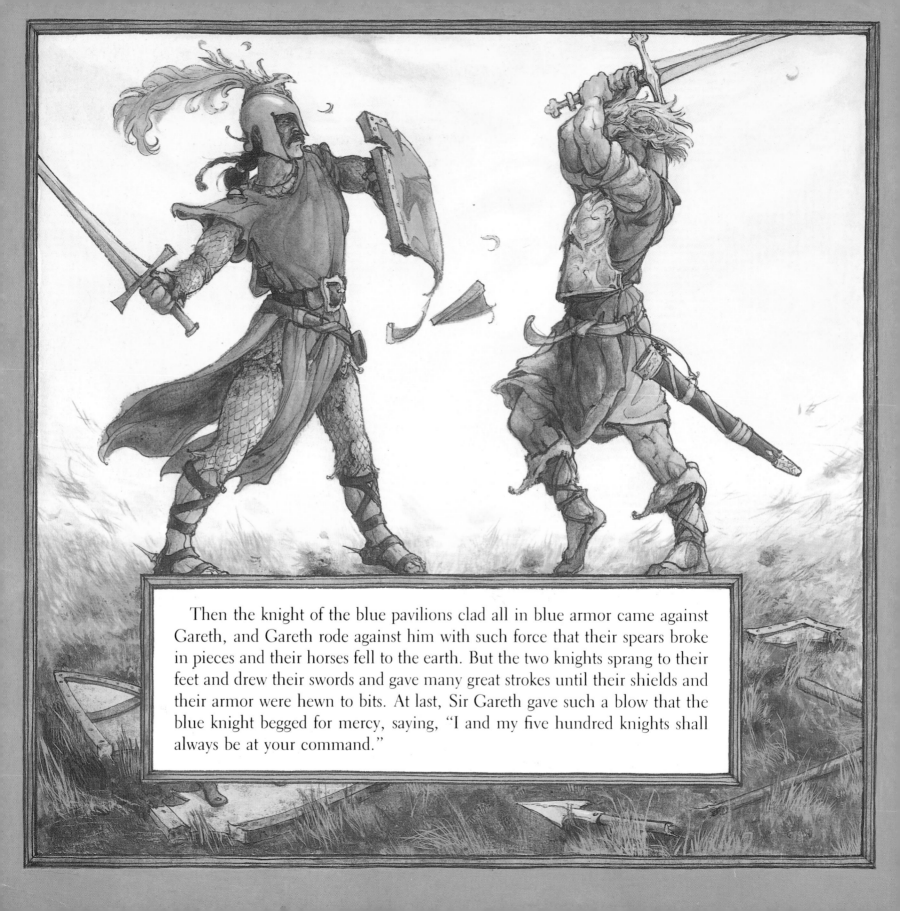

Then the knight of the blue pavilions clad all in blue armor came against Gareth, and Gareth rode against him with such force that their spears broke in pieces and their horses fell to the earth. But the two knights sprang to their feet and drew their swords and gave many great strokes until their shields and their armor were hewn to bits. At last, Sir Gareth gave such a blow that the blue knight begged for mercy, saying, "I and my five hundred knights shall always be at your command."

Then he made Gareth and the lady welcome in his own pavilion and Sir Gareth told how he was going to fight against the Red Knight of the Red Plain to relieve the fair lady's sister.

The blue knight answered, "The Knight of the Red Plain is the most fearsome and perilous knight now living." And he asked the lady, "Is it not your sister Linesse who is besieged by the Red Knight? Is not your name Linette?"

"All this is true," she said.

Then Gareth and Linette rode on together until they came close to the Castle Perilous, and they saw that from the branch of a sycamore tree nearby there hung a great ivory horn.

"Fair sir," said Linette, "if any knight blows this horn, the Red Knight will come to do battle. His strength increases until midday, so do not blow the horn before high noon."

"I will fight him at his strongest," said Sir Gareth, and he blew the horn so eagerly that the Castle Perilous rang with the sound, and those within looked over the walls and out the windows. Then the Red Knight armed himself, and all was blood-red—his armor, spear, and shield—and he rode to a little valley close by the castle so that all within and without might see the battle.

Linette pointed to a far window in a tower of the castle, and said, "Yonder is my sister Linesse."

Sir Gareth said, "Even from afar, she seems a fair lady. I will gladly do battle for her." Then he raised his hand to her and in her far window the lady raised her hand to him.

But the Red Knight called to Sir Gareth, "Look not at her but at me. She is my lady and I have fought many battles for her."

"I think it was a waste of labor," said Gareth. "To love one who does not love you is great folly. I will rescue her or die in the attempt."

"Talk no more with me," said the Red Knight. "Make yourself ready."

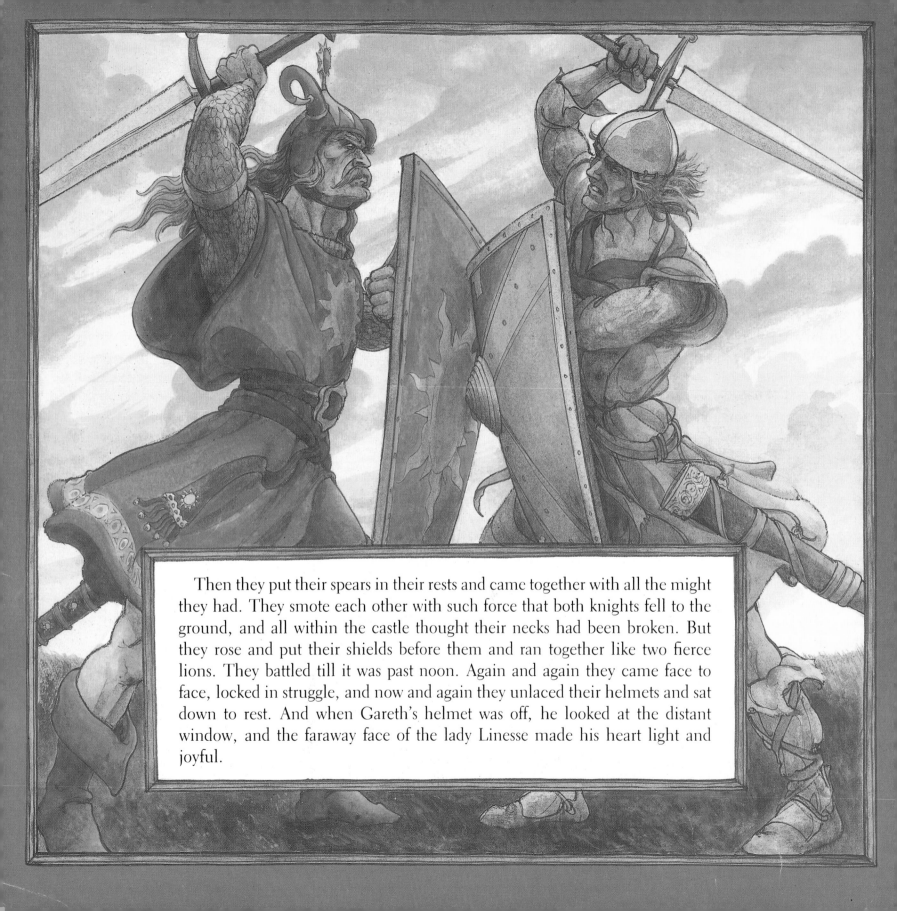

Then they put their spears in their rests and came together with all the might they had. They smote each other with such force that both knights fell to the ground, and all within the castle thought their necks had been broken. But they rose and put their shields before them and ran together like two fierce lions. They battled till it was past noon. Again and again they came face to face, locked in struggle, and now and again they unlaced their helmets and sat down to rest. And when Gareth's helmet was off, he looked at the distant window, and the faraway face of the lady Linesse made his heart light and joyful.

At last the Red Knight smote Gareth such a blow that Gareth lost his sword and fell to the ground.

Then Linette cried out, "Sir Gareth, what has become of your courage? My sister is watching you."

When Gareth heard that, he leaped to his feet and picked up his sword. He struck the sword from the Red Knight's hand and smote him on the helmet so that he fell, and Gareth pinned him to the earth. Then the Red Knight asked for mercy, and many of his noble knights came to Sir Gareth and begged him to spare the life of the Red Knight. "For," said they, "his death will not help you, and his misdeeds cannot be undone. Therefore let him right the wrongs he has done, and we will all be your men."

"Fair lords," said Gareth, "I will release him. But let him yield himself to the lady of the castle."

"This I will do," said the Red Knight, and he went to the castle to ask forgiveness of the lady Linesse. She received him kindly. But when Gareth went to the castle, she sent a message to the gateway, saying, "Go your way, Sir Knight, until I know more of you."

Then secretly she sent a knight to follow Gareth and to capture the dwarf so that she could question him.

Sir Gareth rode away with his dwarf sorrowfully. They rode here and there, and knew not where they rode, until it was dark night. Then, weary and sick at heart for love of the faraway lady, he gave his horse into the care of the dwarf and lay down to rest with his head on his shield.

And while Gareth slept, the knight sent by the lady came softly behind the dwarf. He picked him up and rode away with him as fast as ever he might. But the dwarf cried out to Sir Gareth for help. And Sir Gareth awoke and followed them through marsh and moor until he lost sight of them. Many times his horse and he plunged over their heads in deep mire, for he did not know his way. And while Sir Gareth was in such danger, the dwarf was telling the lady Linesse that her unknown champion was Sir Gareth of Orkney, nephew of King Arthur.

When at last Gareth found the castle again, he was angry, and he drew his sword, shouting to the guards that they must give back his dwarf.

The lady Linesse said, "I would speak with Sir Gareth, but he must not know who I am." Then the drawbridge was let down and the gate was opened. And when Sir Gareth rode in, his dwarf came to take the horse.

"Oh, little fellow," said Sir Gareth, "I have been in much danger for your sake."

He washed, and the dwarf brought him clothing fit for a knight to wear. And when Gareth went into the great hall, he saw the lady Linesse disguised as a strange princess. They exchanged many fair words and kind looks. And Gareth thought, "Would to God that the faraway lady of the tower might prove to be as fair as this lady!"

They danced together, and the lady Linesse said to herself, "Now I know that I would rather Sir Gareth were mine than any king or prince in this world, and if I may not have him as my husband, I will have none. He is my first love, and he shall be the last."

And she told him that she was the same lady he had done battle for, and the one who had caused his dwarf to be stolen away "to know certainly who you were."

Then into the dance came Linette, who had ridden with him along so many perilous paths, and Sir Gareth took the lady Linesse by one hand and Linette by the other, and he was more glad than ever before.

Thus ends the tale of Sir Gareth of Orkney.

NOTE ON THE TEXT

The Kitchen Knight retells the first part of "The Tale of Sir Gareth of Orkney," one of the most exciting and entertaining of the stories about King Arthur and his knights. These legends, drawn from ancient sources, were first woven together and written in English by Sir Thomas Malory during his years as a "knight prisoner" in London's Newgate prison. In 1485 William Caxton edited and printed Malory's book as *Le Morte D'Arthur.* For more than four hundred years Caxton was our chief source for the Arthurian tales in the English language. This changed in 1934 when Walter Oakeshott, then Headmaster of England's famous Winchester school, found a medieval manuscript in one of the school libraries. He was later knighted for his "services to medieval literature" in recognizing that the Winchester manuscript was an important new source for Malory scholars. The Winchester text was edited by Eugène Vinaver and published in 1954. Margaret Hodges consulted both the Caxton and Winchester texts for her retelling of *The Kitchen Knight.*